MIDSUMMER MAYHEM

Written and Illustrated by Shoo Rayner

Dug's Bronze Age Family

Dug   **Woof**

Over 3,000 years ago, Dug's family lived
in the southwest of Britain. They had no
clocks or calendars in those days. Join
Dug as he learns how to tell which day
is Midsummer's Day.

Mini   **Dad**

Chapter One

"There it is!" Dug cheered. He pointed to

the tiny dot of light on the horizon.

"I saw the Midsummer sun first!"

"Well done!" said Dad. "Happy Midsummer!"

Flames flickered and wood crackled as they lit the celebration bonfire. The warm sun rose slowly in the sky. Dug's family decorated the Sunstone with ivy and flowers. Woof chased sparks.

"How do you know it's Midsummer, Dad?"
Dug asked.

"Well ... it's just something you know," said
Dad.

"But how?" Dug insisted.

"It's like this," Dad explained. "In winter, the sun comes up over there. Everyday, the sun moves along a little bit until, at Midsummer, it comes up over here. Then it goes all the way back again to winter."

"But how exactly do you know which day is Midsummer?" asked Dug.

"Because when you stand with your back to the Sunstone," said Dad, "the sun comes up over here!"

"Where?" asked Dug.

"Where those birds are!" Dad pointed, but the birds flew away.

"I mean … over there by the oxen," Dad grumbled. The oxen ran off to drink at the river's edge.

Dug picked up a stick.

"Today, I noticed that the sun came up behind this clump of grass. If I push this stick in the ground, we can remember it for next year."

"That's a brilliant idea, son!" said Dad.

"Ruff!" Woof pulled the stick out of the ground and ran away with it.

"Here's a better stick," said Dad. "Really bash it into the ground so Woof can't take it away."

Chapter Two

Two days later, and three sticks were bashed in the ground.

"Finally!" said Dad. "The sun is on it's journey back to winter."

"You mean that yesterday was really Midsummer and not two days ago when you said it was!" Dug folded his arms. Dad nodded and looked embarrassed. "We'll probably have bad luck all year now."

"But now we know where to look next year, don't we?" Dug said, brightly. "I marked it."

"If we're going to stop the bad luck," said Dad, "we'll have to mark the dawn every day until Midwinter."

"We're going to need more sticks," said Dug.

Dad cut sticks from the trees with his big axe and Dug sharpened the ends with his little axe.

Woof grabbed the sticks and ran away with them. "Ruff! Ruff!" Mini chased after her. "Come back you!"

The days grew shorter and colder. Early every morning, Dad stood by the Sunstone. When the sun rose, he told Dug where to put a stick to mark the sunrise.

Then, one icy morning, when Dug thought his fingers would freeze into blocks of ice, the sun turned on its journey back to summer.

"Light the bonfire!" said Dad. "Happy Midwinter everyone!"

Chapter Three

"We won't be needing these." Dug picked

up the rest of the sticks they'd made. Woof

grabbed one. "Woof! No!"

Dug tripped and fell on the sticks.

"Ooh! Ah! Ooh! Eeh! Ooh! Ow!" Dug

bumped down the hill. He rolled along

on the sticks, as if he was floating across

the frosty grass!

"Ha! ha!" Dad laughed. "That gives me a great idea, son. You are so clever!"

He led Dug to the river to explain the idea.

"Look at these two stones," Dad said. "We can use them to mark Midsummer's Day. Those sticks won't last forever."

"But they're so heavy!" said Dug. "We can't carry them!"

"We'll roll them on sticks," Dad smiled. "Just like you rolled down the hill. But we need bigger rollers."

Dad chopped down trees with his big axe and Dug chopped them into logs with his little axe.

Woof tried stealing a log but it was too heavy. "Silly Woof!" said Mini.

Chapter Four

"Put that branch under the big stone and rest it on a smaller stone," said Dad. "Now pull it down with all your strength."

"Nnnnngh!" Dug grunted. "Hey! I'm lifting the stone all by myself!"

Dad smiled, slipping some logs under the stone. "You can lift most things with a good strong lever," he said.

Dug and Mini helped Dad tie up the oxen. They tied the wooden beam, called a yoke, to the stone using long ropes.

"If we put logs in front of the stone, we can roll it onto them," said Dad. "Then we can keep using the logs that are left behind to put in front again."

"Pull!" Dug and Mini told the oxen. The beasts moved forward and Dad kept placing logs in front of the stones. Woof was snapping at the feet of the oxen.

"The stone is moving!" Dug cheered. "We'll have it up by the Sunstone in no time."

"Then we can go back for the other one," laughed Dad.

Chapter Five

Dad drew a line in the dust between the
Sunstone and the stick that marked where
the sun rose on Midsummer's Day.
"Let's get digging!" said Dad. They made
holes on either side of the line for the stones
to stand in.

The oxen pulled the stones upright in the holes.

"They look magnificent!" said Dug.

"They certainly do!" said Dad, proudly.

It was nearly dawn on Midsummer's Day. Dug, Dad and Mini waited by the Sunstone. "There it is!" shouted Dug. He pointed at a tiny dot of light on the horizon. "I saw the Midsummer sun first!"

The two tall stones stood like sentries. They cast long shadows as the golden-red sun rose in the sky. The first rays of sunlight squeezed through the gap between the stones. Then the narrow beam of light ran across the grass and up the Sunstone, lighting the shining bronze sun at the top.

"Perfect!" cheered Dug. "Now we will always know that today is Midsummer's day!"

"It's good luck for us all!" said Dad. "Happy Midsummer, everyone!" Flames flickered and crackled as they lit the celebration bonfire. The warm sun rose slowly in the sky.

"Ruff! Ruff!" Woof chased sparks while Dug, Dad and Mini decorated the Sunstone with ivy and flowers.

Bronze Age Facts

There were no clocks in the Bronze Age. People knew the time of day by measuring where the sun was in the sky. They went to bed at sunset and woke up at sunrise. There were no calendars either, but in places like Stonehenge, the sun could be used to tell the time of year. One of the great mysteries is how the stones were transported such great distances — perhaps on rollers or by Oxen (cattle).

Franklin Watts
First published in Great Britain in 2016 by
The Watts Publishing Group

Text and Illustrations © Shoo Rayner 2016

Series Editor: Melanie Palmer
Series Advisor: Catherine Glavina
Series Designers: Peter Scoulding
and Cathryn Gilbert

ISBN 978 1 4451 4800 7 (hbk)
ISBN 978 1 4451 4802 1 (pbk)
ISBN 978 1 4451 4801 4 (library ebook)

Printed in China

MIX
Paper from
responsible sources
FSC® C104740

FSC
www.fsc.org

Franklin Watts
An imprint of
Hachette Children's Group
Part of The Watts Publishing Group
Carmelite House
50 Victoria Embankment
London EC4Y 0DZ

An Hachette UK Company
www.hachette.co.uk

www.franklinwatts.co.uk